CANCELLED

young justice ™

3

STONE ARCH BOOKS
a capstone imprint

STONE ARCH BOOKS™

Published in 2013
A Capstone Imprint
1710 Roe Crest Drive
North Mankato, MN 56003
www.capstonepub.com

Originally published by DC Comics in the U.S. in single magazine form as Young Justice #8.

DC Comics
1700 Broadway, New York, NY 10019
A Warner Bros. Entertainment Company

Printed in China by Nordica.
0413/CA21300442
032013 007226NORDF13

Cataloging-in-Publication Data is available at the Library of Congress website:
ISBN: 978-1-4342-6040-6 (library binding)

Summary: Can someone with Artemis's pedigree really be a hero? A close encounter when the team takes action against the deadly android Amazo may give her the chance to prove herself if she can survive the onslaught of Professor Ivo's malevolent MONQIs!

STONE ARCH BOOKS

Ashley C. Andersen Zantop *Publisher*
Michael Dahl *Editorial Director*
Donald Lemke & Sean Tulien *Editors*
Heather Kindseth *Creative Director*
Brann Garvey & Alison Thiele *Designers*
Kathy McColley *Production Specialist*

DC COMICS

Scott Peterson & Jim Chadwick *Original U.S. Editors*
Michael McCalister *U.S. Assistant Editor*
Mike Norton *Cover Artist*

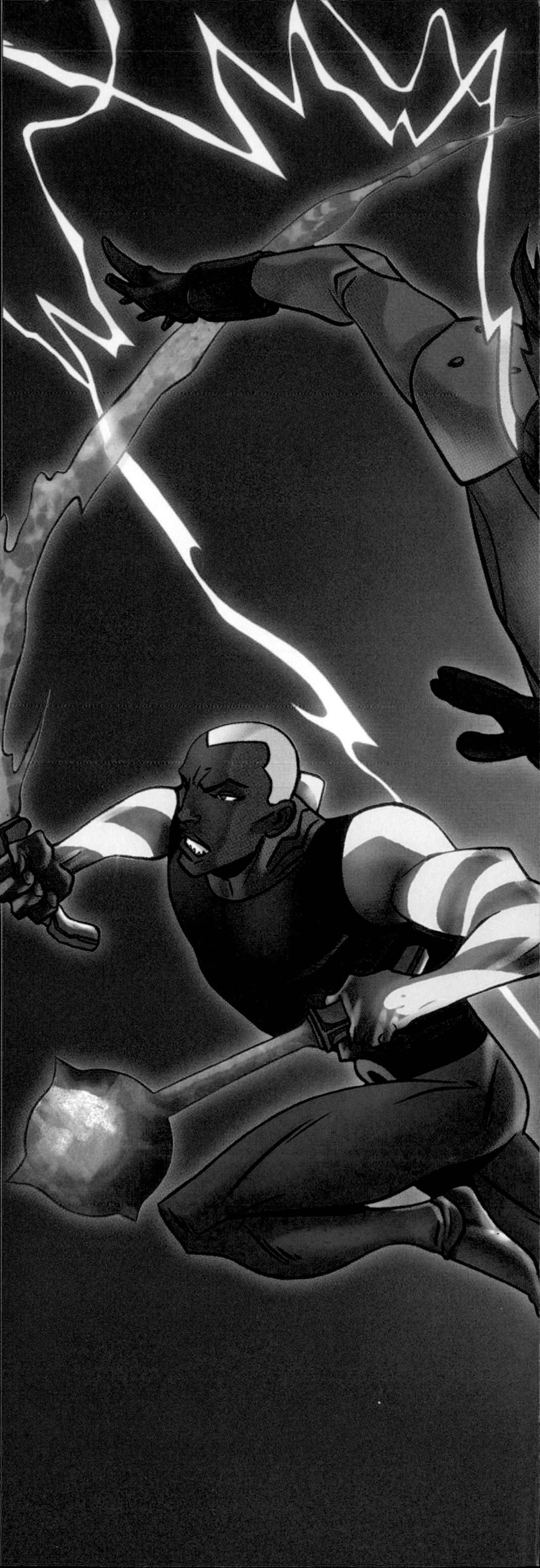

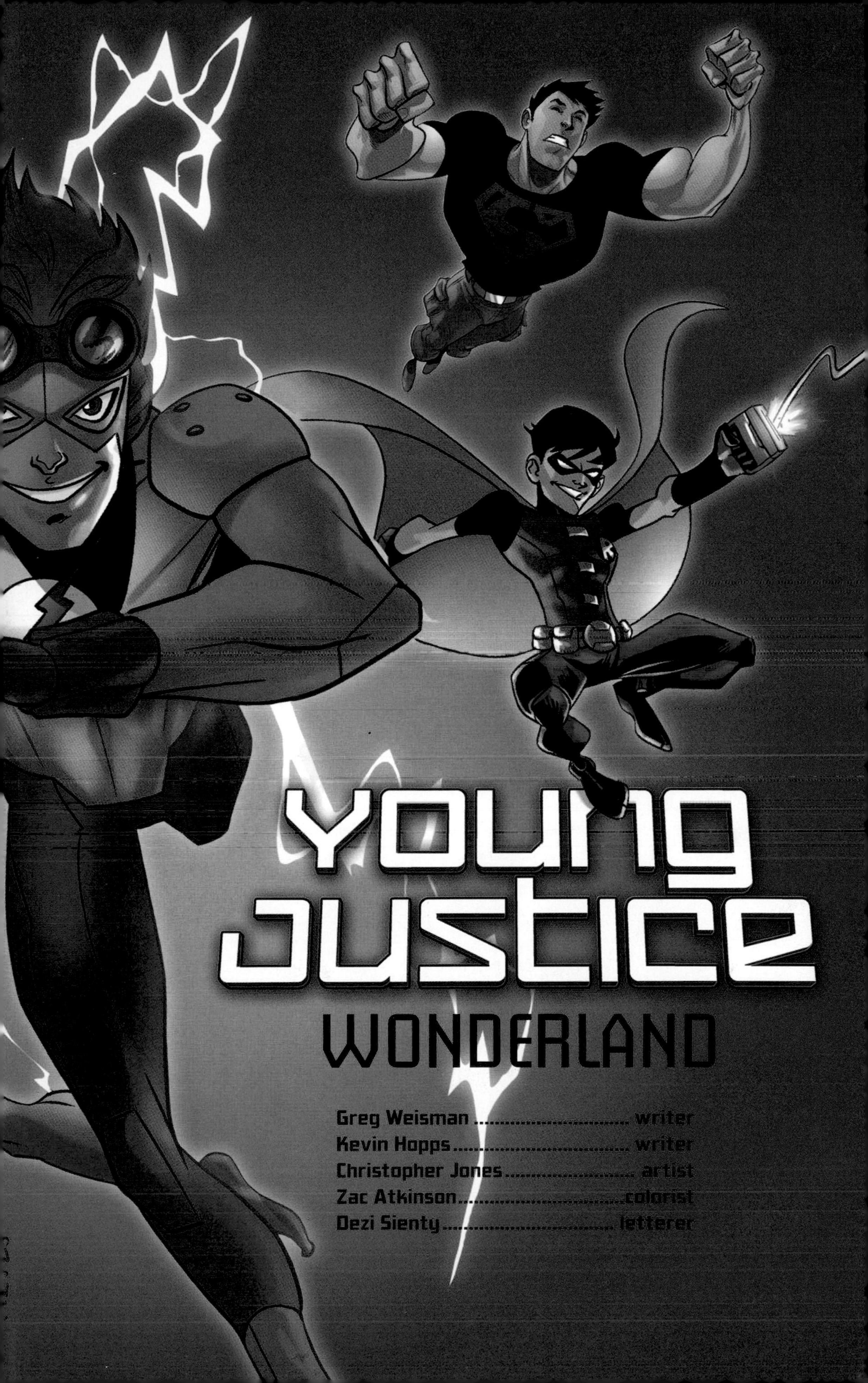

YOUNG JUSTICE
WONDERLAND

Greg Weisman .... writer
Kevin Hopps .... writer
Christopher Jones.......................... artist
Zac Atkinson....................................colorist
Dezi Sienty .... letterer

YOUNG JUSTICE

AQUALAD

AGE: 16   **SECRET IDENTITY:** Kaldur' Ahm

BIO: Aquaman's apprentice; a cool, calm warrior and leader; totally amphibious with the ability to bend and shape water.

SUPERBOY

AGE: 16   **SECRET IDENTITY:** Conner Kent

BIO: Cloned from Superman; a shy and uncertain teenager; gifted with super-strength, infrared vision, and leaping abilities.

ARTEMIS

AGE: 15   **SECRET IDENTITY:** Classified

BIO: Green Arrow's niece; a dedicated and tough fighter; extremely talented in both archery and martial arts.

KID FLASH

AGE: 15   **SECRET IDENTITY:** Wally West

BIO: Partner of the Flash; a competitive team member, often lacking self-control; gifted with super-speed.

ROBIN

AGE: 13   **SECRET IDENTITY:** Dick Grayson

BIO: Partner of Batman; the youngest member of the team; talented acrobat, martial artist, and hacker.

MISS MARTIAN

AGE: 16   **SECRET IDENTITY:** M'gann M'orzz

BIO: Martian Manhunter's niece; polite and sweet; ability to shape-shift, read minds, transform, and fly.

THE STORY SO FAR...

Artemis has spotted the Young Justice team members fighting a mysterious battle with a swirling, strange foe and a barrel of robotic monkeys...

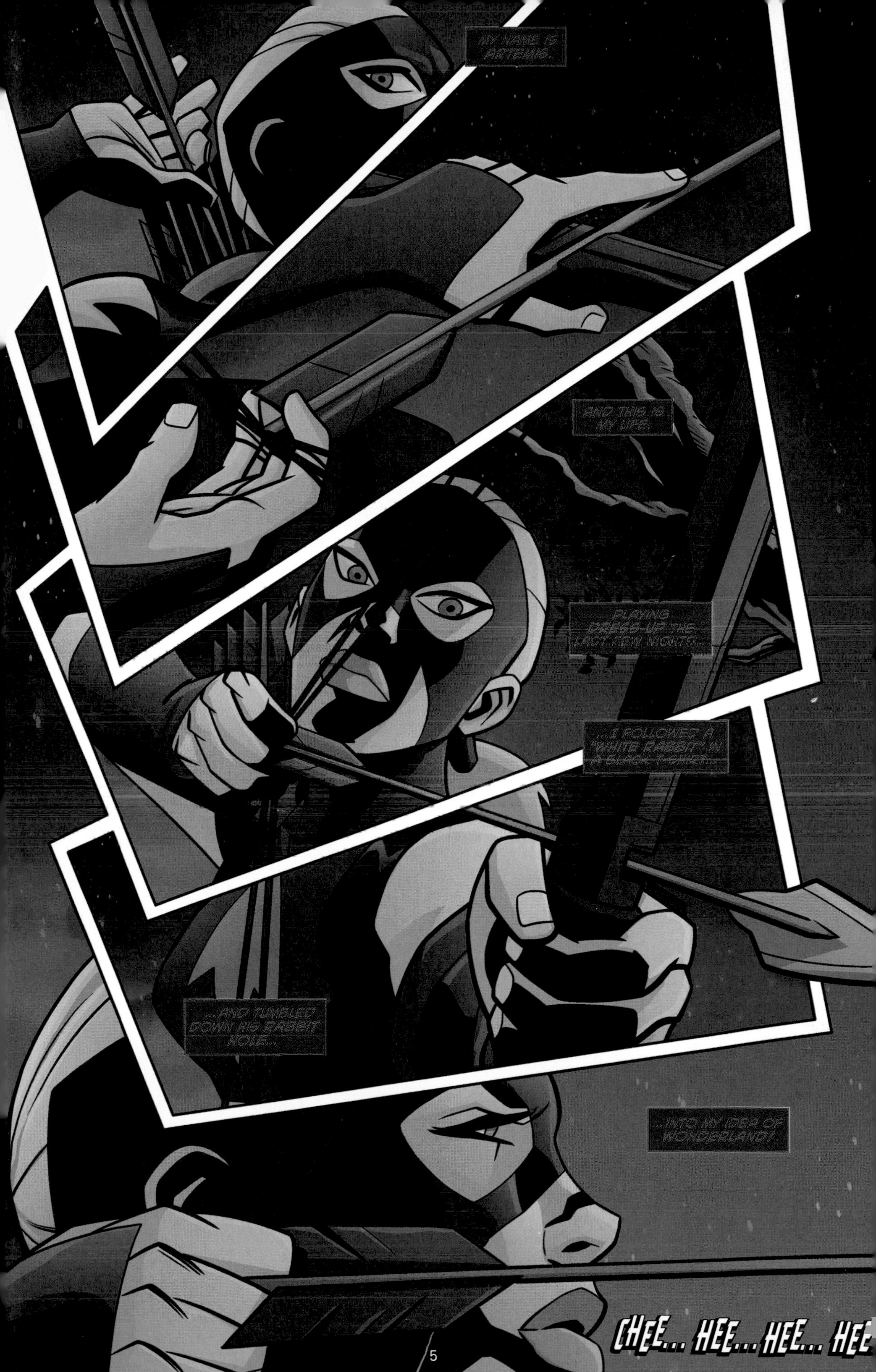
MY NAME IS ARTEMIS.
AND THIS IS MY LIFE.
PLAYING DRESS-UP THE LAST FEW NIGHTS...
...I FOLLOWED A "WHITE RABBIT" IN A BLACK T-SHIRT...
...AND TUMBLED DOWN HIS RABBIT HOLE...
...INTO MY IDEA OF WONDERLAND!
CHEE... HEE... HEE... HEE

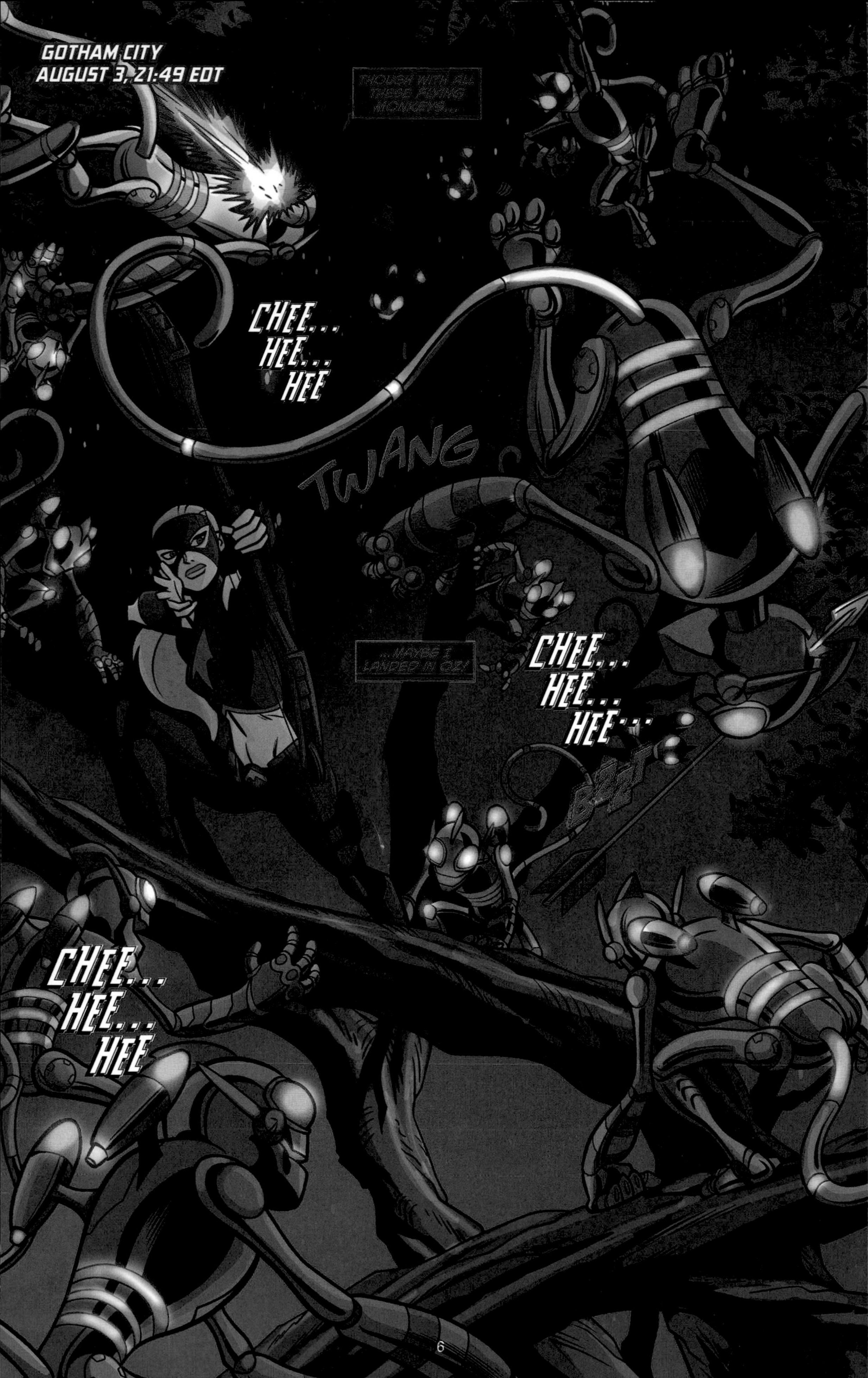

GOTHAM CITY
AUGUST 3, 21:49 EDT
THOUGH WITH ALL THESE FLYING MONKEYS...
CHEE... HEE... HEE
TWANG
...MAYBE I LANDED IN OZ!
CHEE... HEE... HEE...
CHEE... HEE... HEE

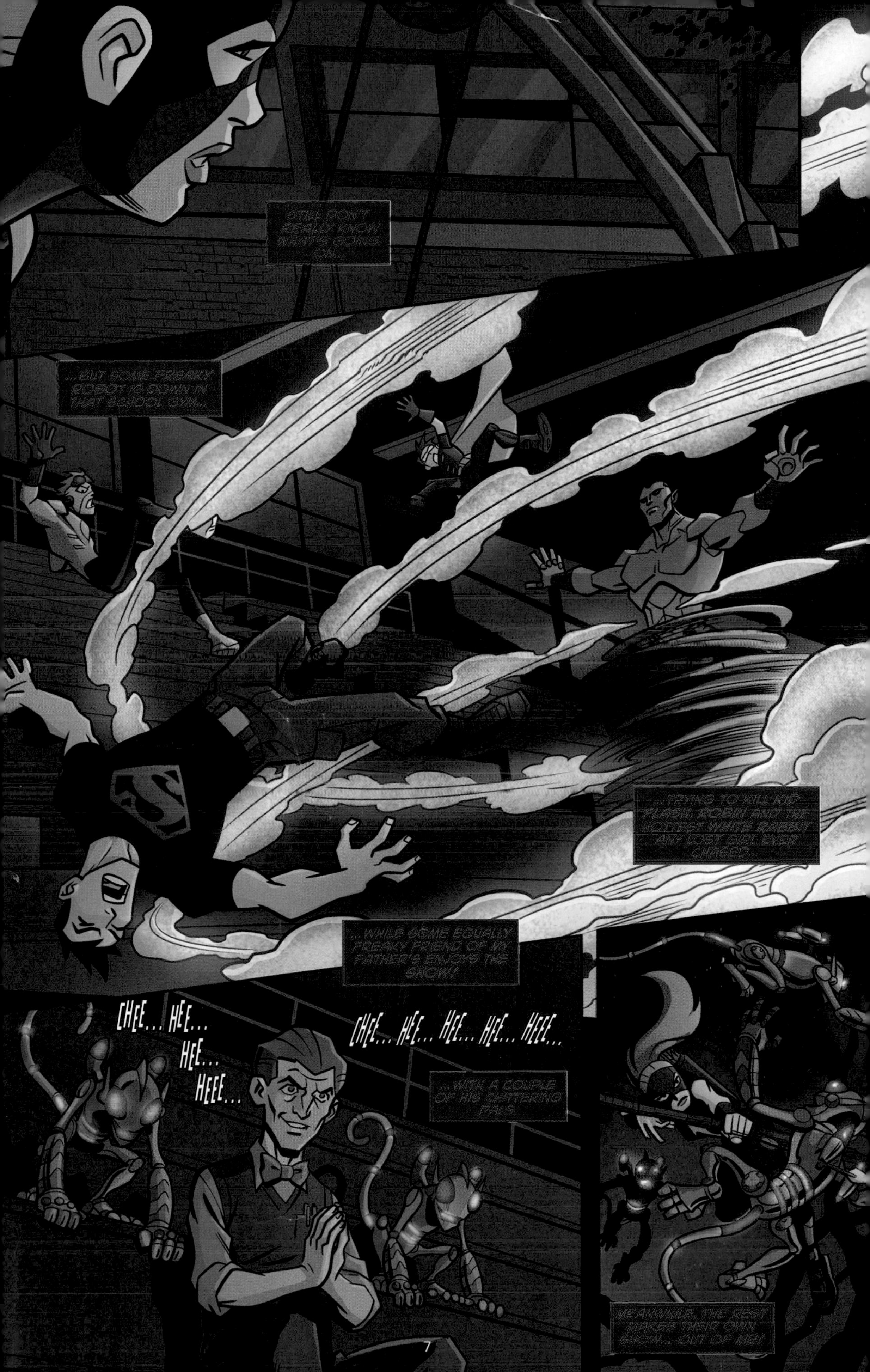
STILL DON'T REALLY KNOW WHAT'S GOING ON...
...BUT SOME FREAKY ROBOT IS DOWN IN THAT SCHOOL GYM...
...TRYING TO KILL KID FLASH, ROBIN AND THE HOTTEST WHITE RABBIT ANY LOST GIRL EVER CHASED.
...WHILE SOME EQUALLY FREAKY FRIEND OF MY FATHER'S ENJOYS THE SHOW!
CHEE... HEE... HEE... HEEE...
CHEE... HEE... HEE... HEE... HEEE...
...WITH A COUPLE OF HIS CHATTERING PALS.
MEANWHILE, THE REST MAKES THEIR OWN SHOW... OUT OF ME!

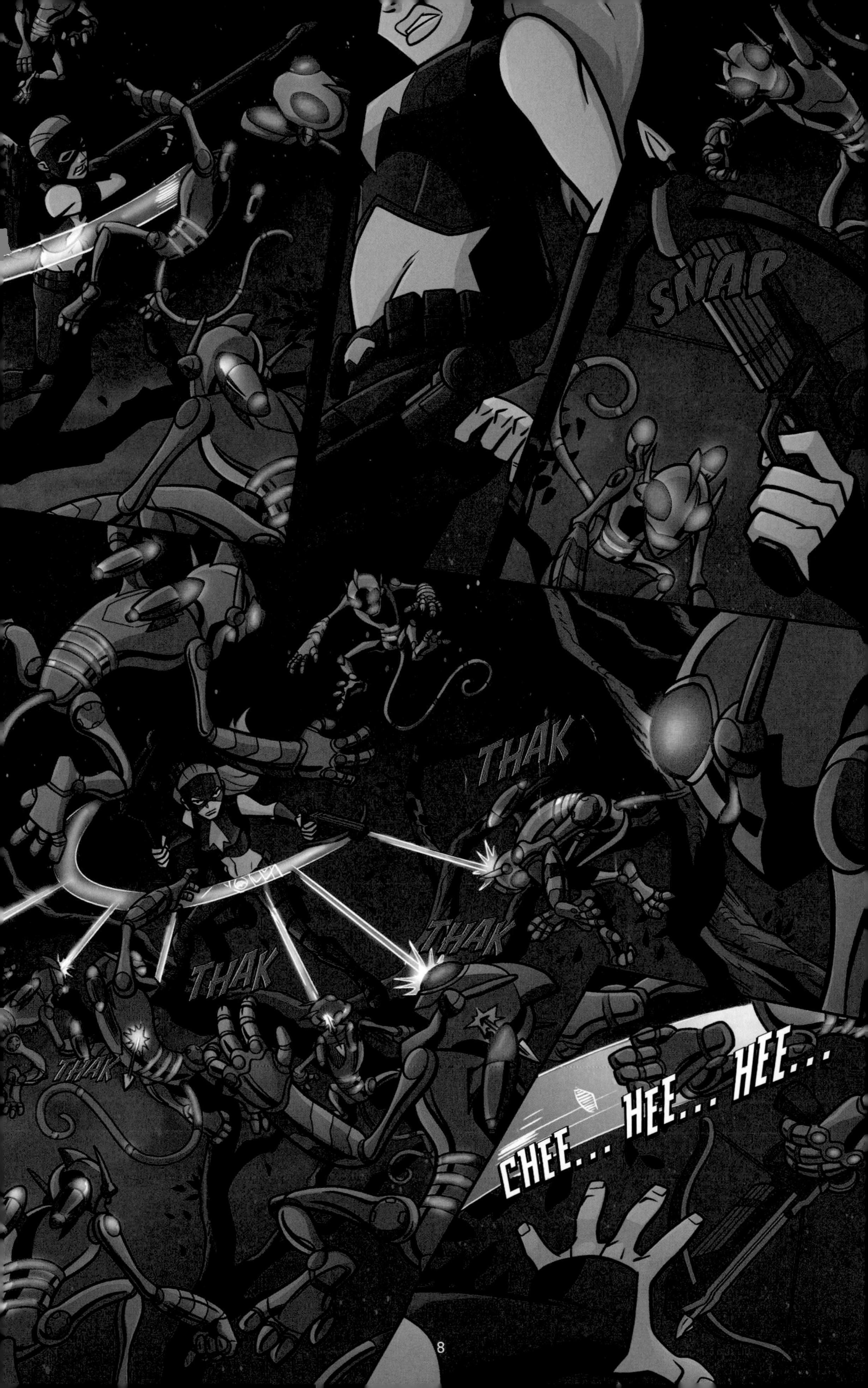
SNAP
THAK
THAK
THAK
THAK
CHEE... HEE... HEE...

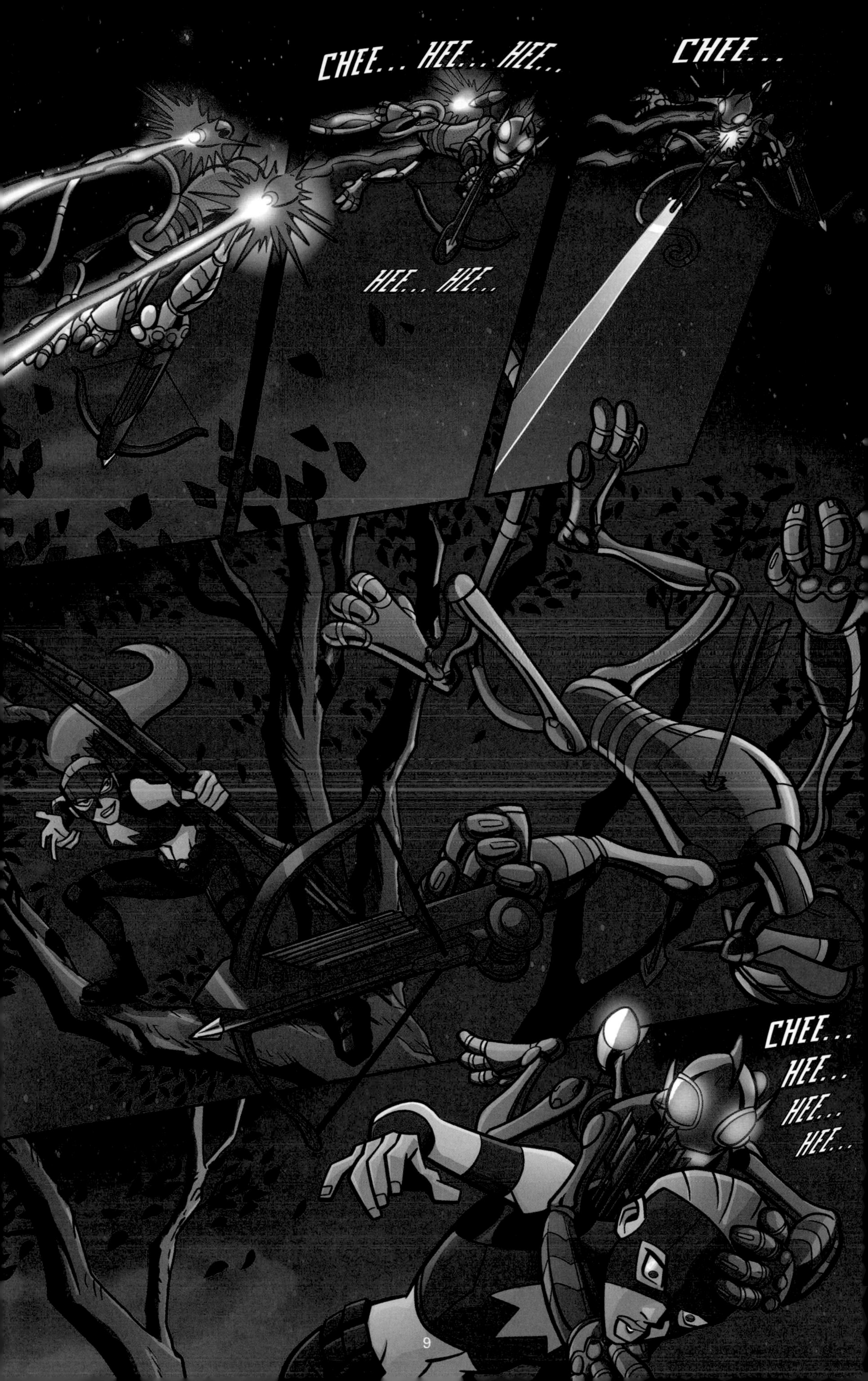
CHEE... HEE... HEE...
CHEE...
HEE... HEE...
CHEE...
HEE...
HEE...
HEE...

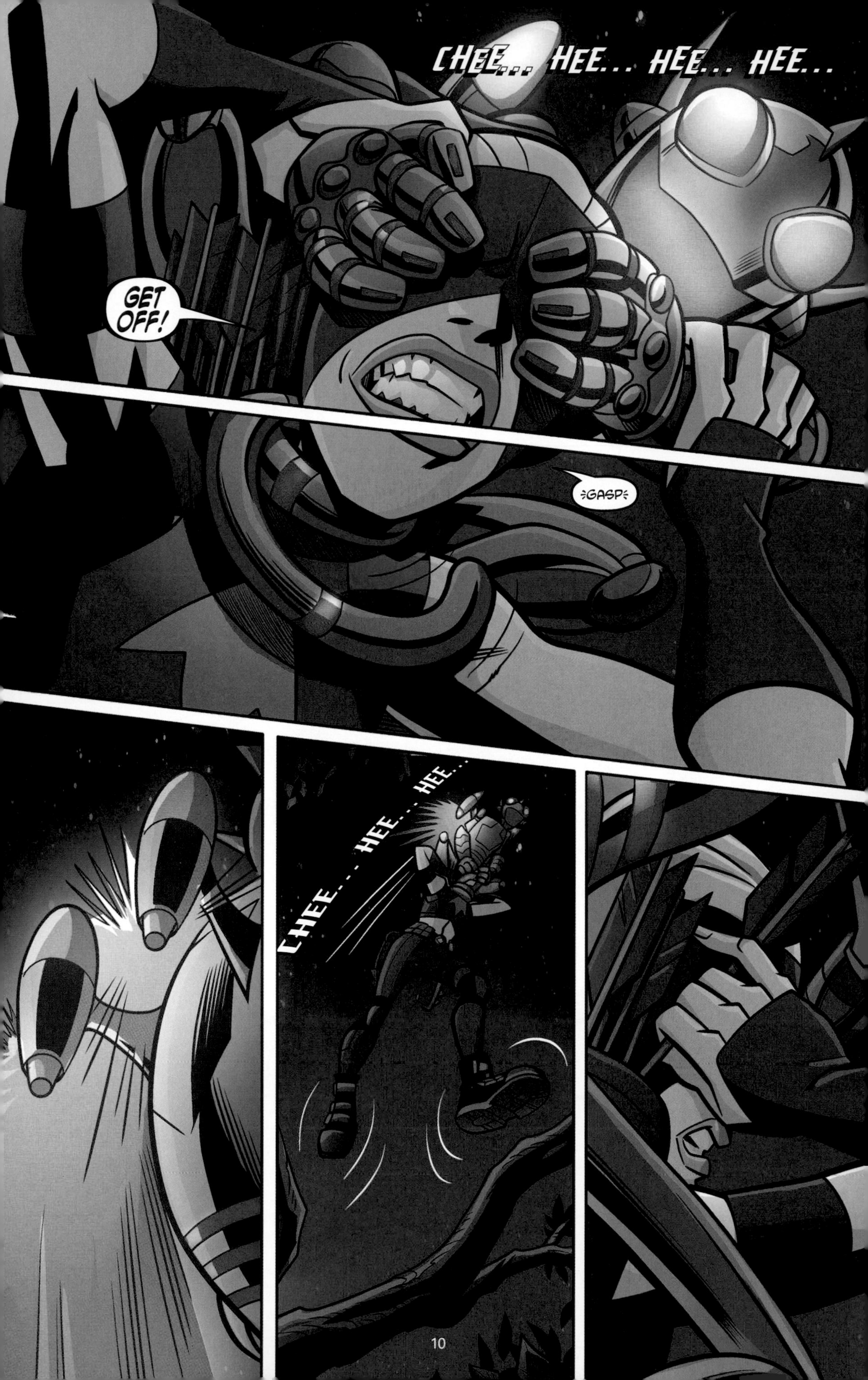
CHEE... HEE... HEE... HEE...
GET OFF!
GASP
CHEE... HEE... HEE...

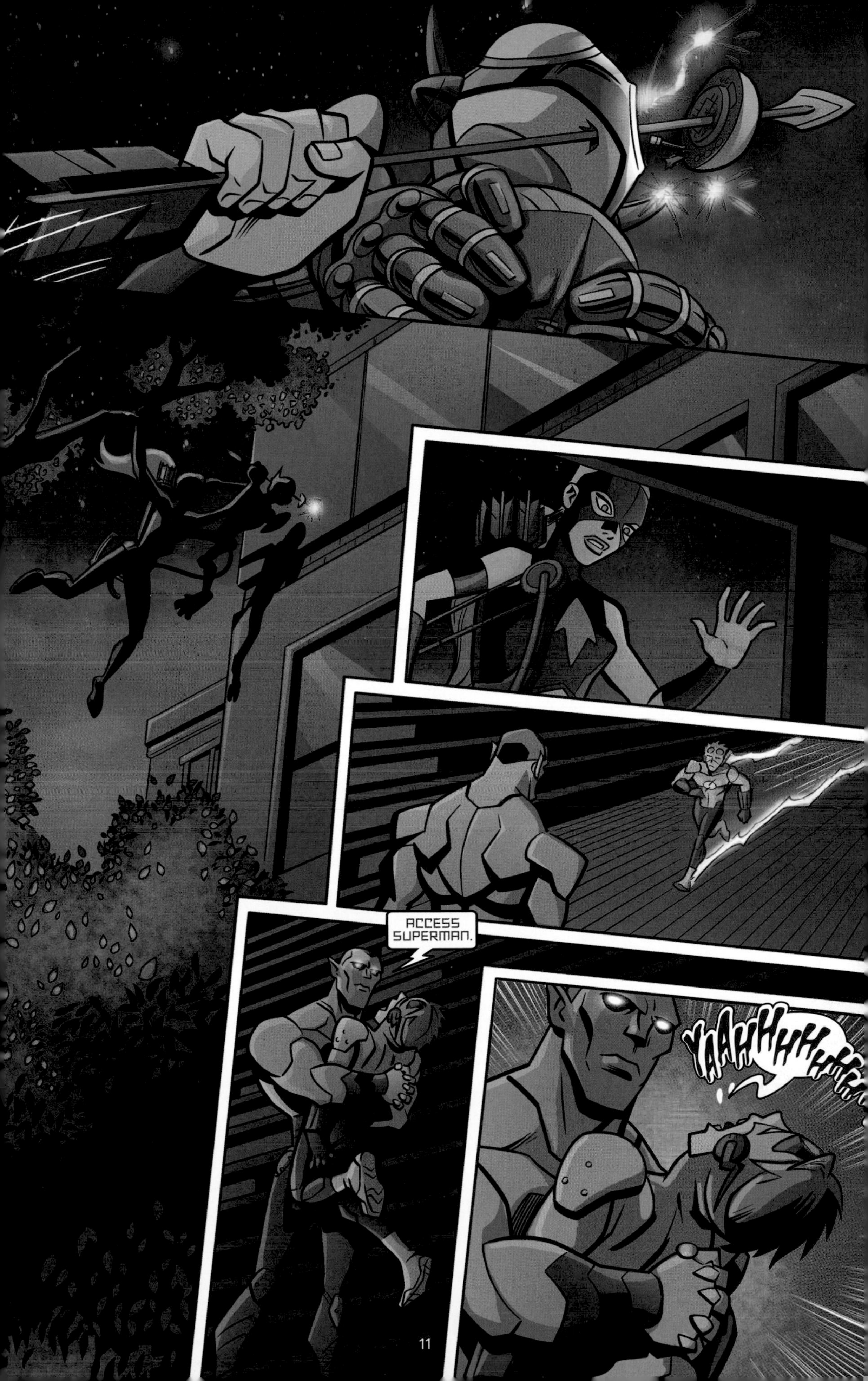
ACCESS SUPERMAN.
YAAHHHHHH

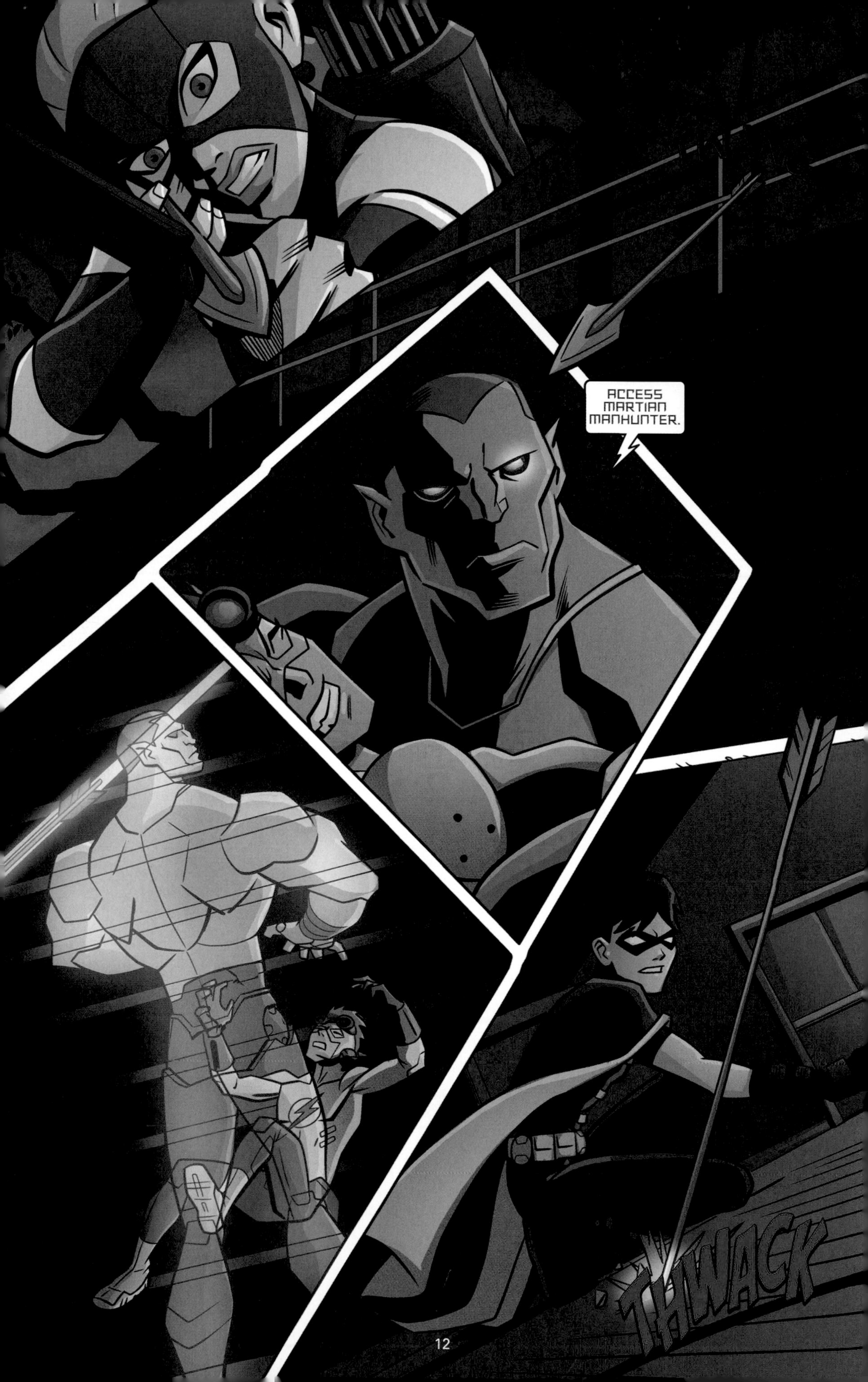
ACCESS MARTIAN MANHUNTER.
THWACK

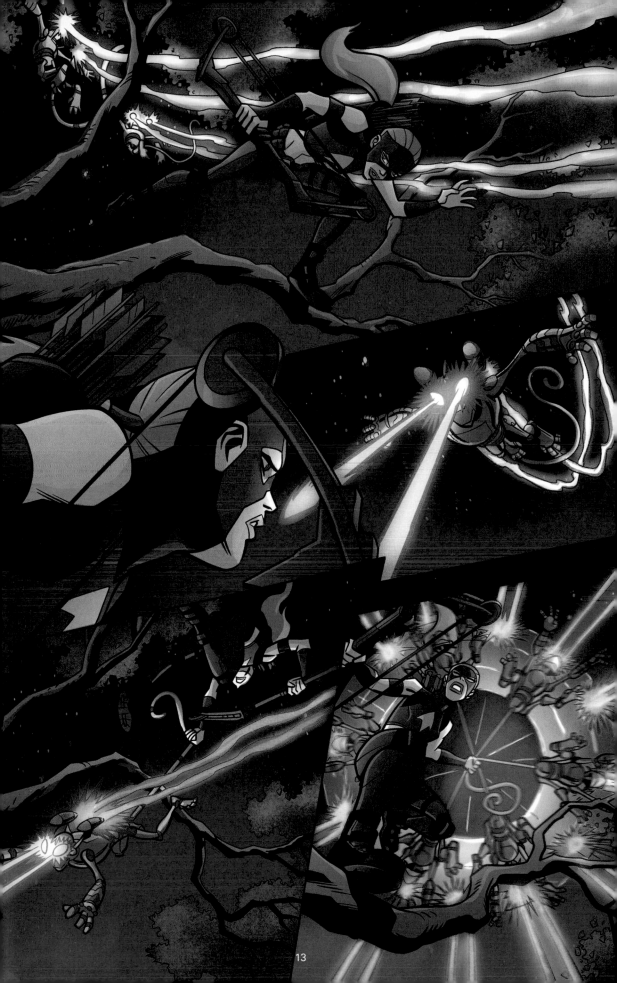

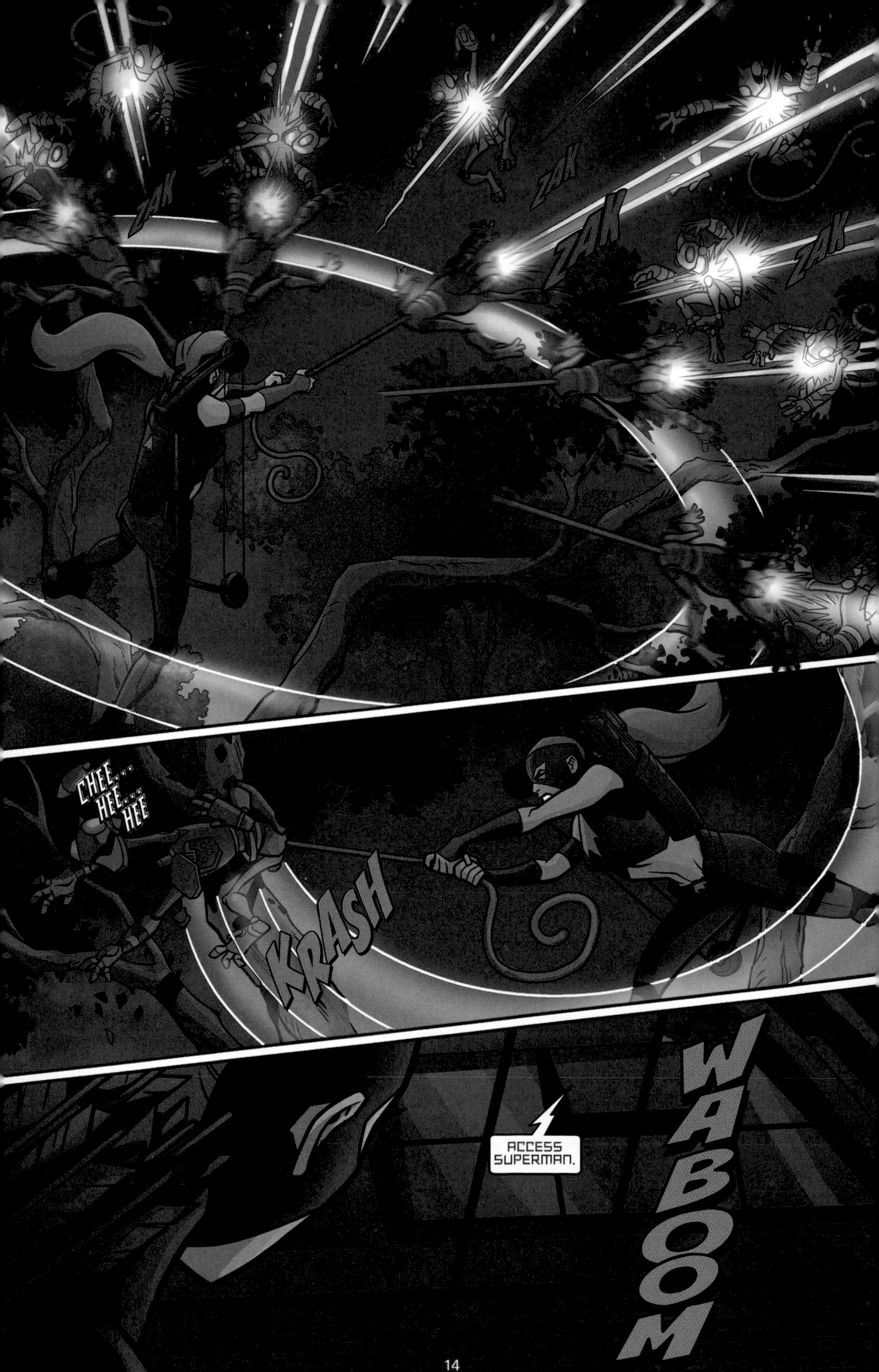
ZAK
ZAK
ZAK
ZAK
ZAK
CHEE... HEE... HEE
KRASH
ACCESS SUPERMAN.
WABOOM

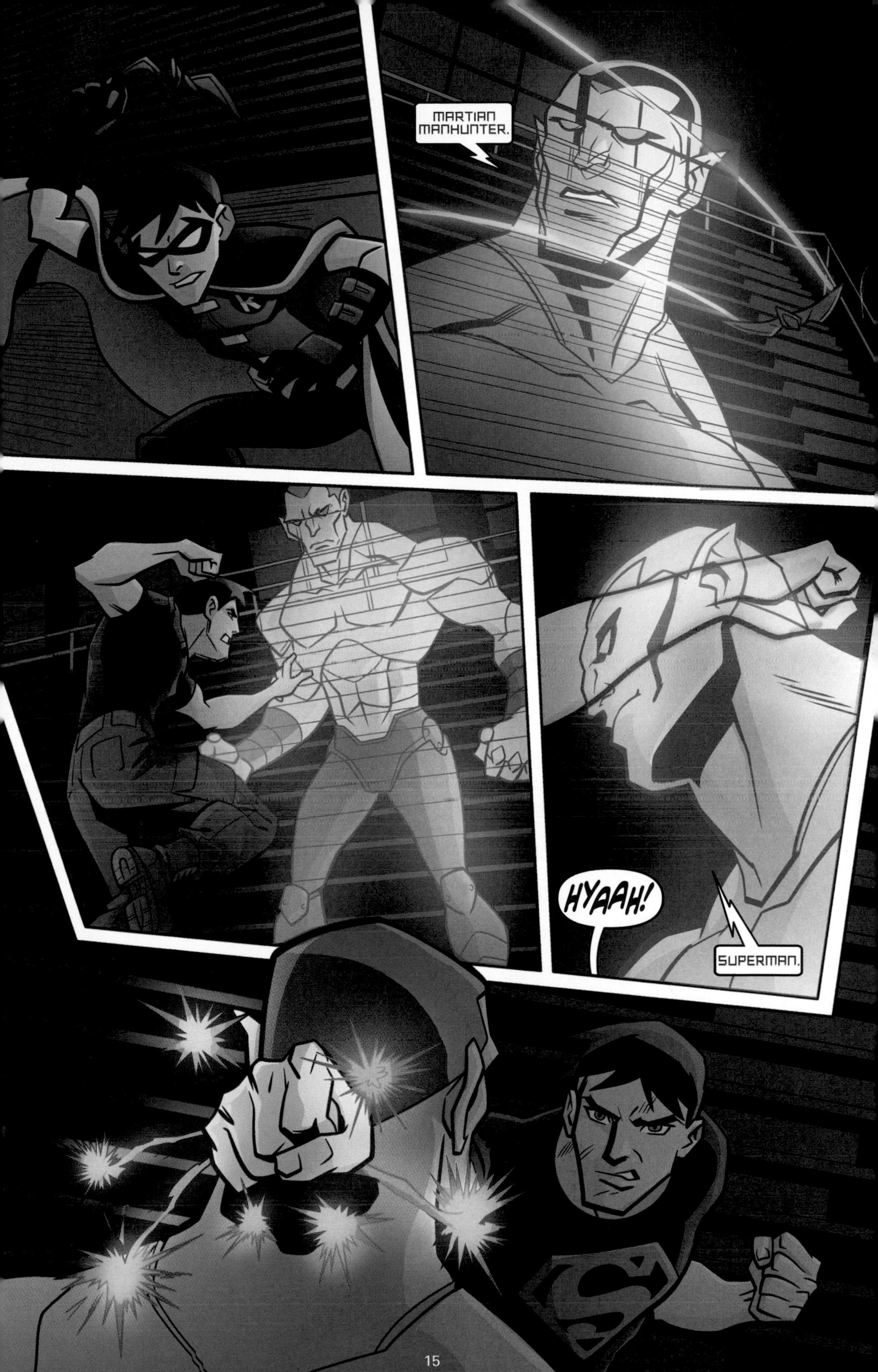
MARTIAN MANHUNTER.
HYAAH!
SUPERMAN.

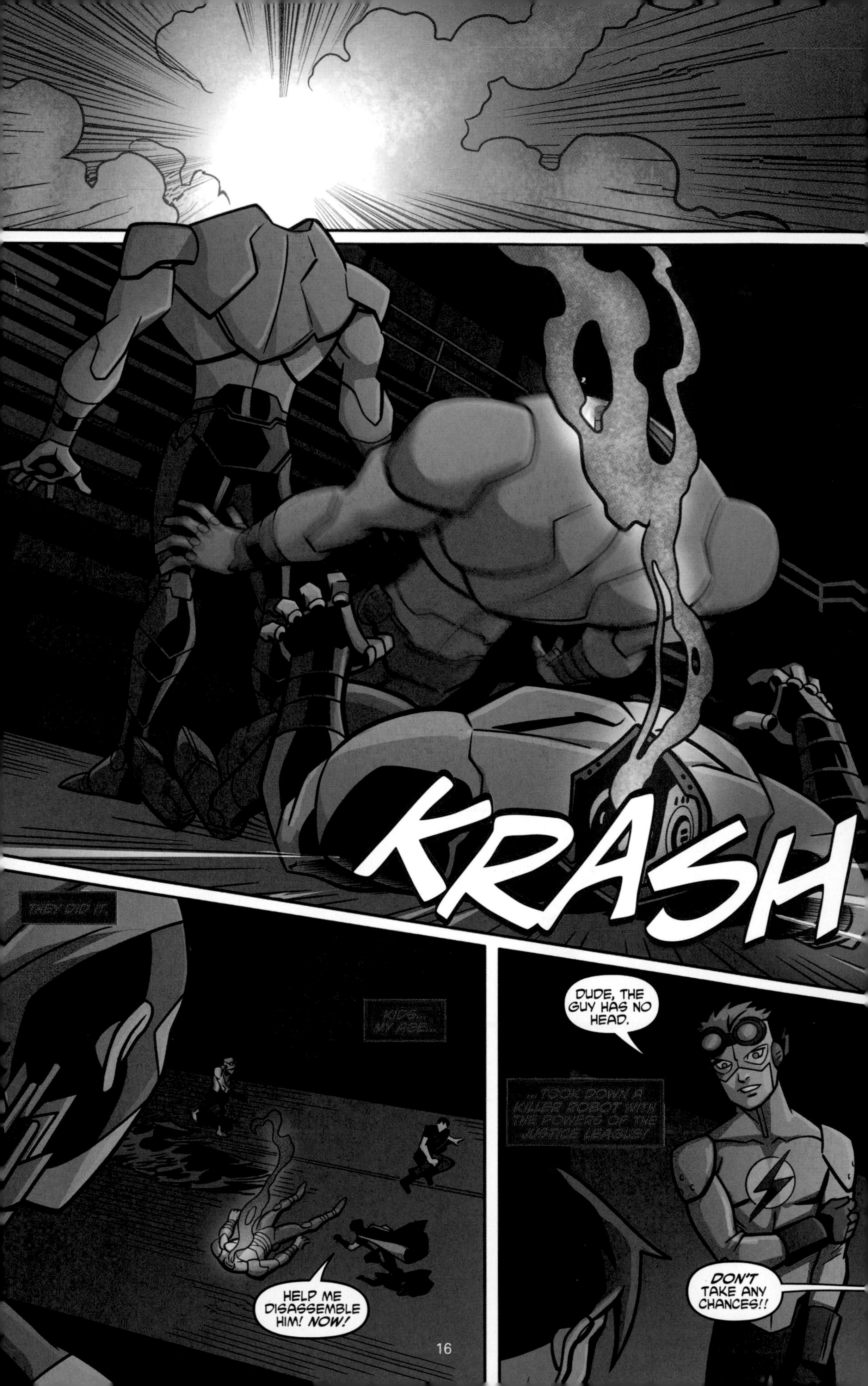
KRASH
THEY DID IT.
KIDS... MY AGE...
HELP ME DISASSEMBLE HIM! NOW!
DUDE, THE GUY HAS NO HEAD.
...TOOK DOWN A KILLER ROBOT WITH THE POWERS OF THE JUSTICE LEAGUE!
DON'T TAKE ANY CHANCES!!

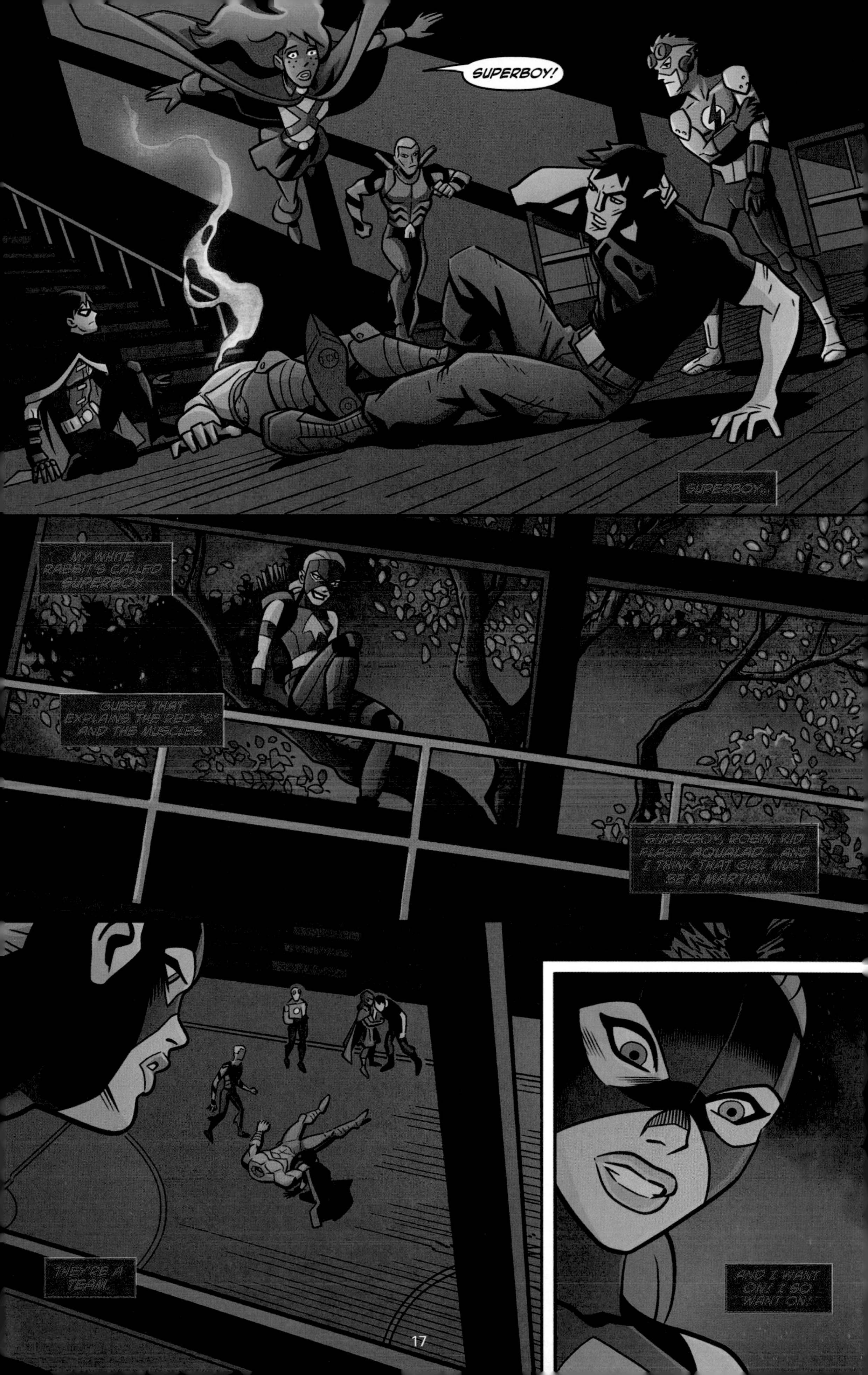
SUPERBOY!
SUPERBOY...
MY WHITE RABBIT'S CALLED SUPERBOY.
GUESS THAT EXPLAINS THE RED "S" AND THE MUSCLES.
SUPERBOY, ROBIN, KID FLASH, AQUALAD... AND I THINK THAT GIRL MUST BE A MARTIAN...
THEY'RE A TEAM.
AND I WANT ON! I SO WANT ON!

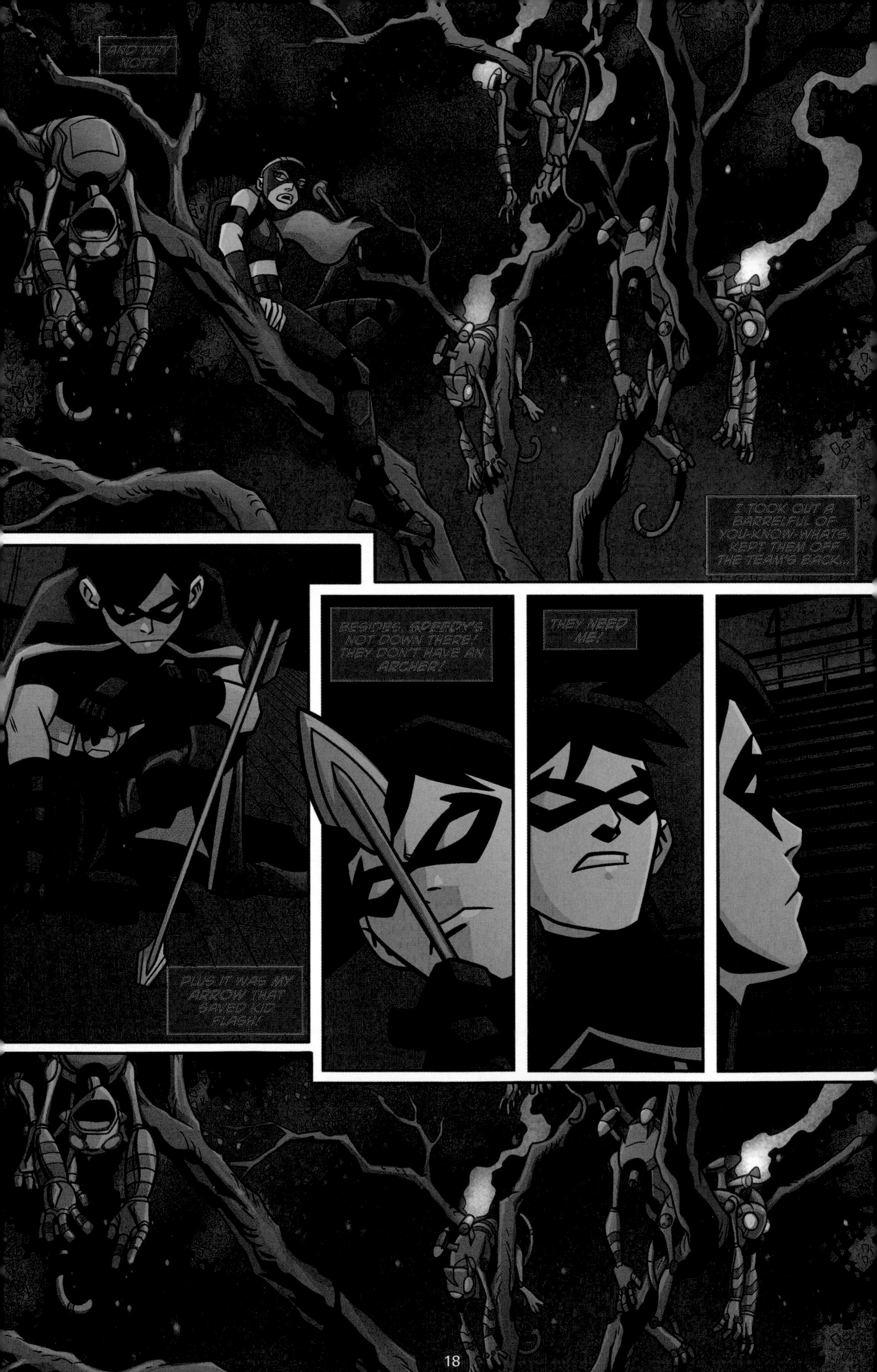
AND WHY NOT?
I TOOK OUT A BARRELFUL OF YOU-KNOW-WHATS, KEPT THEM OFF THE TEAM'S BACK...
PLUS IT WAS MY ARROW THAT SAVED KID FLASH!
BESIDES, SPEEDY'S NOT DOWN THERE! THEY DON'T HAVE AN ARCHER!
THEY NEED ME!

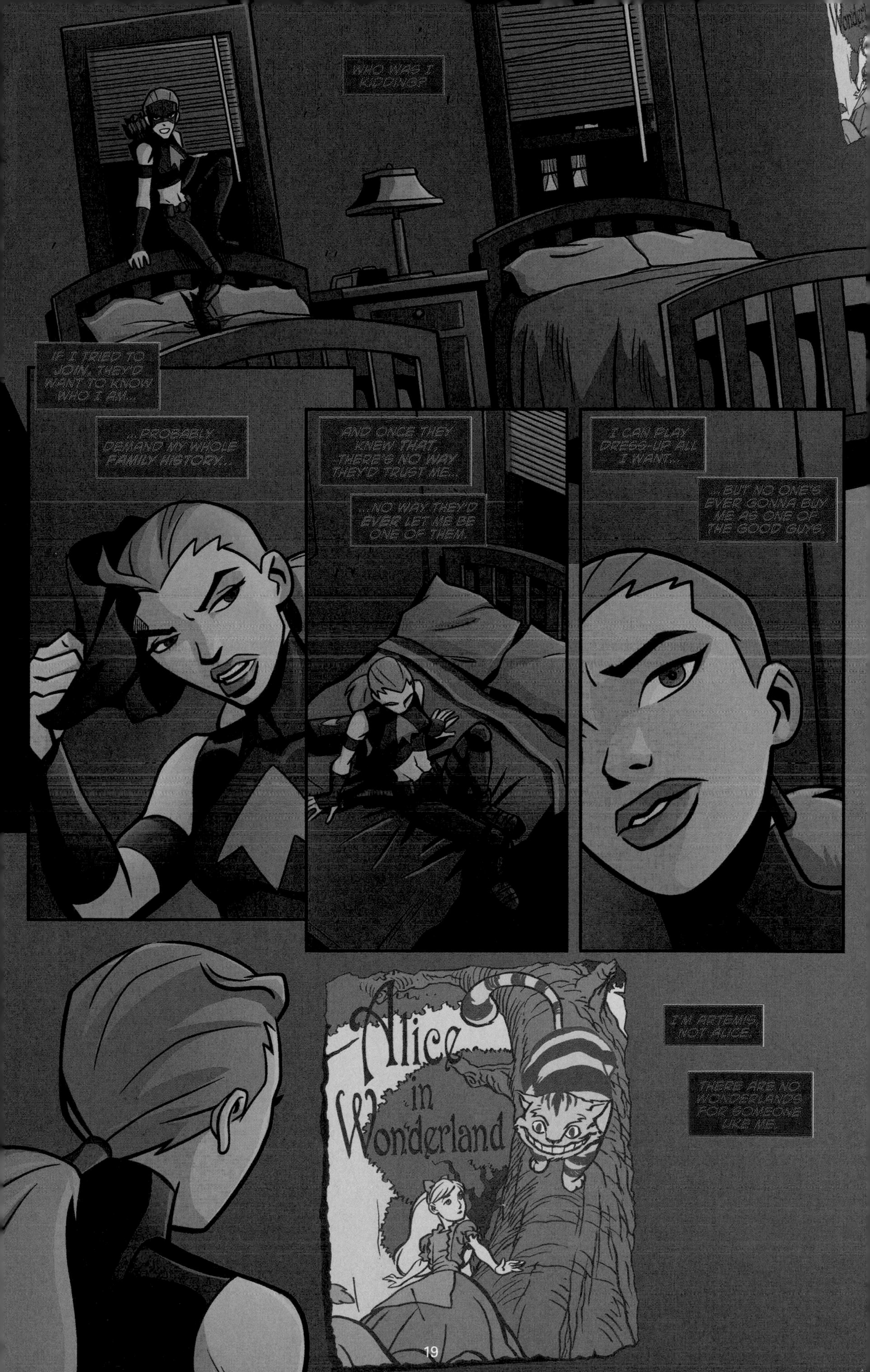
WHO WAS I KIDDING?
IF I TRIED TO JOIN, THEY'D WANT TO KNOW WHO I AM...
...PROBABLY DEMAND MY WHOLE FAMILY HISTORY...
AND ONCE THEY KNEW THAT, THERE'S NO WAY THEY'D TRUST ME...
...NO WAY THEY'D EVER LET ME BE ONE OF THEM.
I CAN PLAY DRESS-UP ALL I WANT...
...BUT NO ONE'S EVER GONNA BUY ME AS ONE OF THE GOOD GUYS.
Alice in Wonderland
I'M ARTEMIS, NOT ALICE.
THERE ARE NO WONDERLANDS FOR SOMEONE LIKE ME.

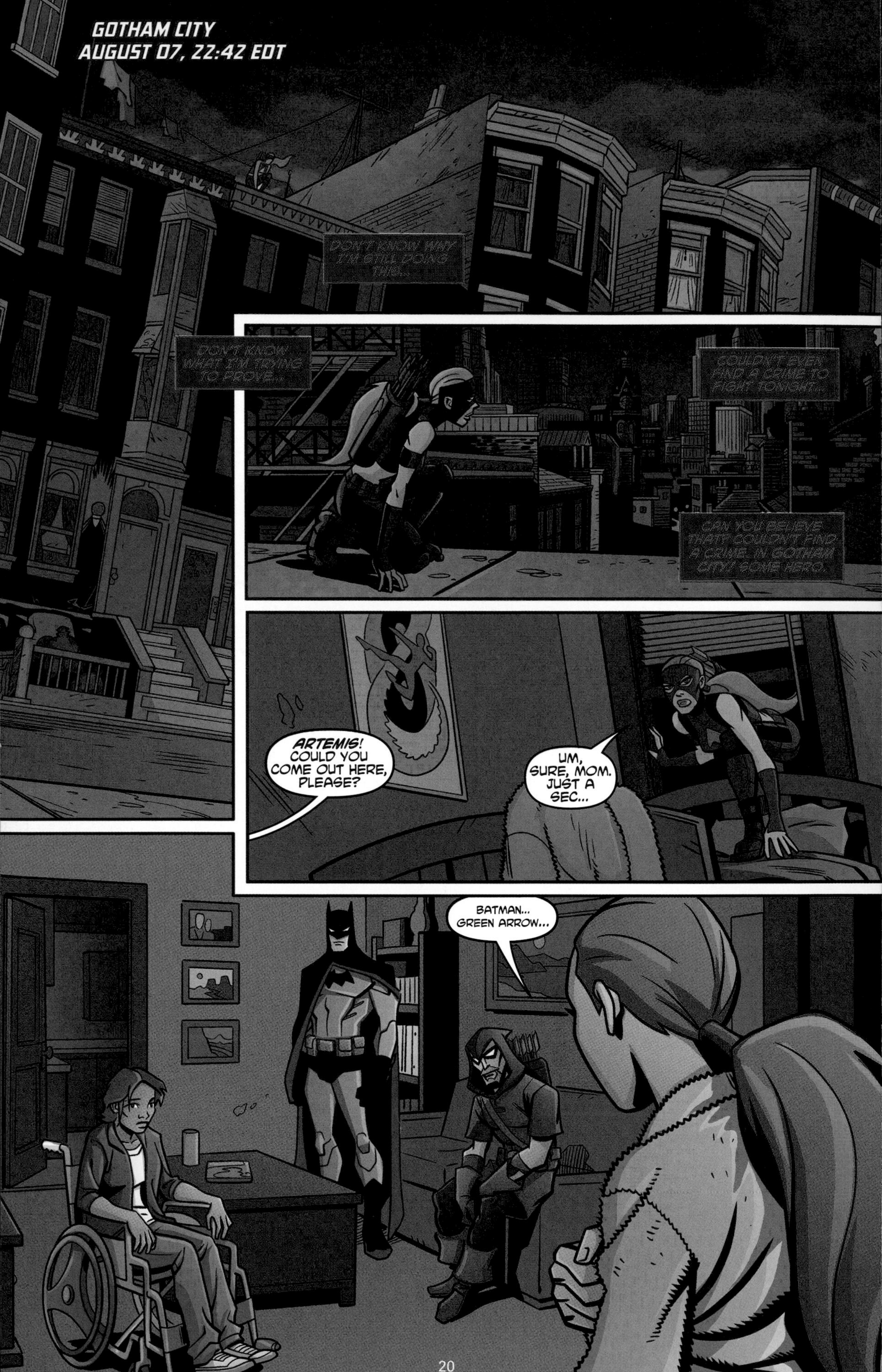
GOTHAM CITY
AUGUST 07, 22:42 EDT
DON'T KNOW WHY I'M STILL DOING THIS...
DON'T KNOW WHAT I'M TRYING TO PROVE...
COULDN'T EVEN FIND A CRIME TO FIGHT TONIGHT...
CAN YOU BELIEVE THAT? COULDN'T FIND A CRIME IN GOTHAM CITY! SOME HERO.
ARTEMIS! COULD YOU COME OUT HERE, PLEASE?
UM, SURE, MOM. JUST A SEC...
BATMAN... GREEN ARROW...

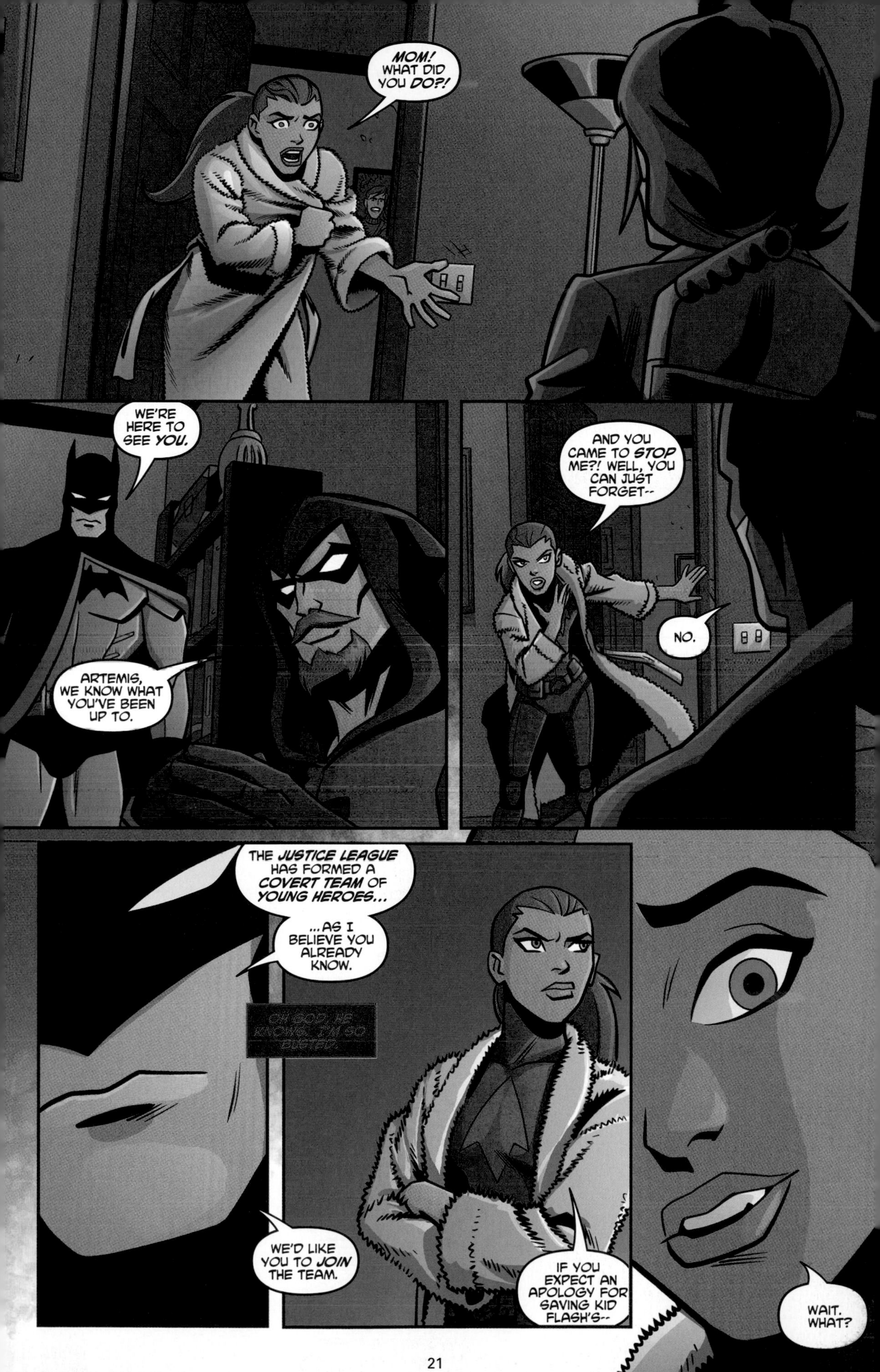
MOM! WHAT DID YOU DO?!
WE'RE HERE TO SEE YOU.
ARTEMIS, WE KNOW WHAT YOU'VE BEEN UP TO.
AND YOU CAME TO STOP ME?! WELL, YOU CAN JUST FORGET--
NO.
THE JUSTICE LEAGUE HAS FORMED A COVERT TEAM OF YOUNG HEROES...
...AS I BELIEVE YOU ALREADY KNOW.
OH GOD, HE KNOWS. I'M SO BUSTED.
WE'D LIKE YOU TO JOIN THE TEAM.
IF YOU EXPECT AN APOLOGY FOR SAVING KID FLASH'S--
WAIT. WHAT?

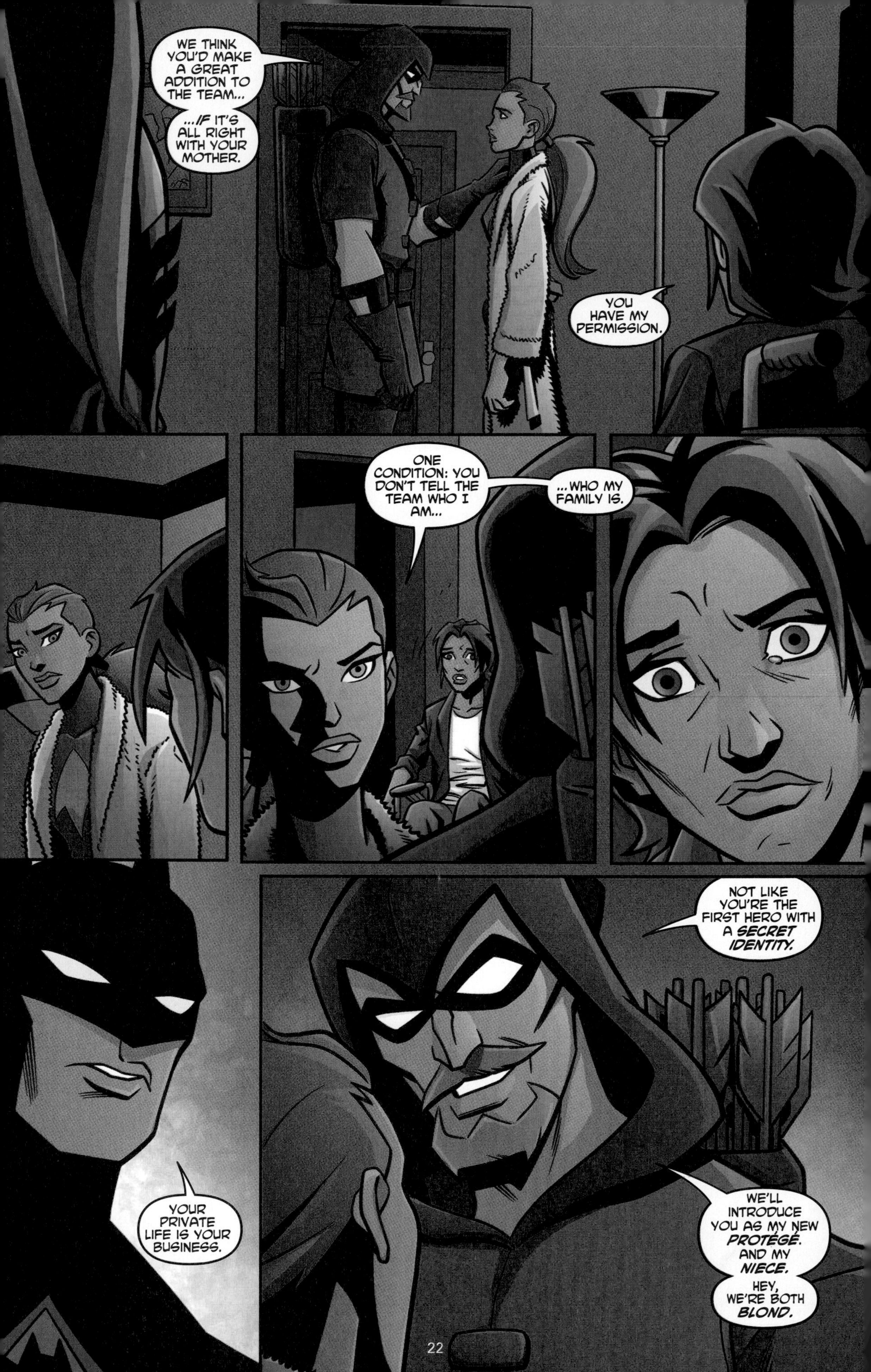
WE THINK YOU'D MAKE A GREAT ADDITION TO THE TEAM...
...*IF* IT'S ALL RIGHT WITH YOUR MOTHER.
YOU HAVE MY PERMISSION.
ONE CONDITION: YOU DON'T TELL THE TEAM WHO I AM...
...WHO MY FAMILY IS.
YOUR PRIVATE LIFE IS YOUR BUSINESS.
NOT LIKE YOU'RE THE FIRST HERO WITH A *SECRET IDENTITY.*
WE'LL INTRODUCE YOU AS MY NEW *PROTÉGÉ*. AND MY *NIECE.*
HEY, WE'RE BOTH *BLOND.*

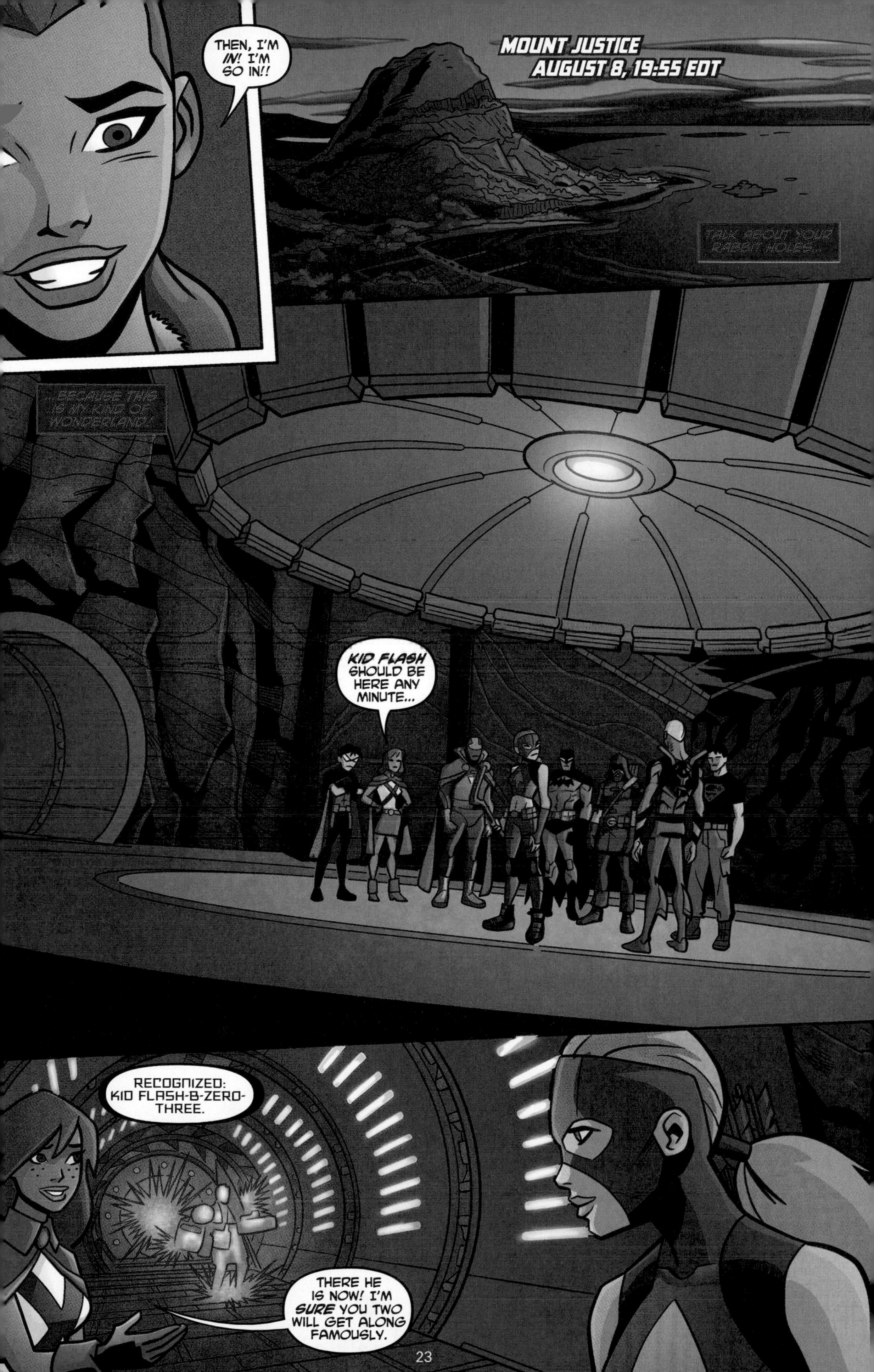
THEN, I'M *IN!* I'M SO IN!!
MOUNT JUSTICE
AUGUST 8, 19:55 EDT
TALK ABOUT YOUR RABBIT HOLES...
...BECAUSE THIS IS MY KIND OF WONDERLAND!
KID FLASH SHOULD BE HERE ANY MINUTE...
RECOGNIZED: KID FLASH-B-ZERO-THREE.
THERE HE IS NOW! I'M *SURE* YOU TWO WILL GET ALONG FAMOUSLY.

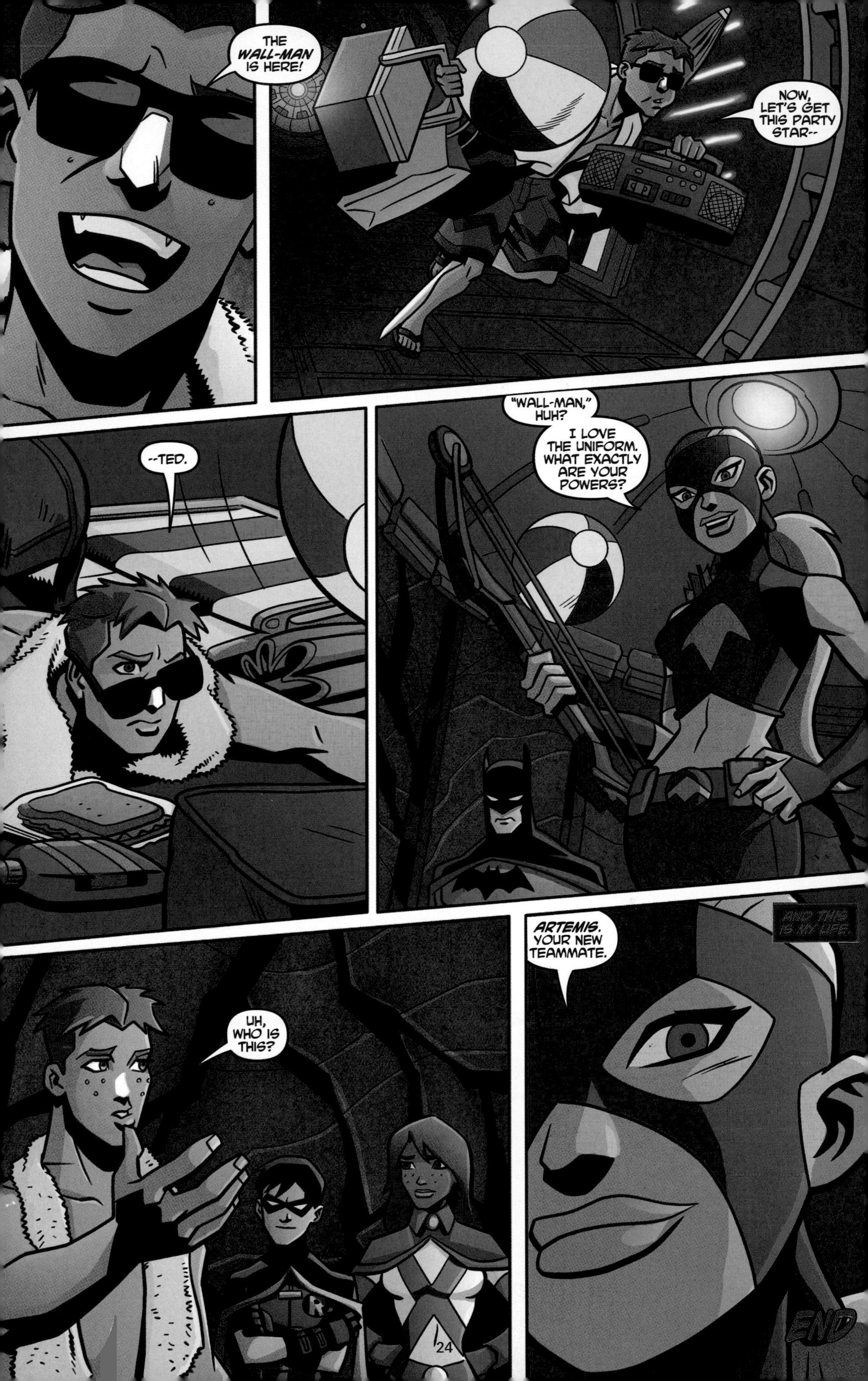
THE *WALL-MAN* IS HERE!
NOW, LET'S GET THIS PARTY STAR--
--TED.
"WALL-MAN," HUH?
I LOVE THE UNIFORM. WHAT EXACTLY ARE YOUR POWERS?
UH, WHO IS THIS?
ARTEMIS. YOUR NEW TEAMMATE.
AND THIS IS MY LIFE.
END

CAN YOUNG JUSTICE TURN THINGS AROUND...?

Read the next action-packed adventure to find out!

only from...

 STONE ARCH BOOKS™

a capstone imprint   www.capstonepub.com

CREATORS

GREG WEISMAN WRITER

Greg Weisman is an American comic book and animation writer. His best-known works for DC Comics include the comic book series Young Justice [as well as the animated series], Max Steel, and several Batman book series.

KEVIN HOPPS WRITER

Kevin Hopps is a staff writer for Young Justice [both the TV series and the comic book series]. He has also written for the Justice League TV series.

CHRISTOPHER JONES ARTIST

Christopher Jones is a professional illustrator and comic book artist. He has worked on Young Justice, The Batman Strikes!, and many other book series for DC Comics.

GLOSSARY

access (AK-sess)--to get information from a computer or database

chittering (CHIT-ur-ing)--twittering or chirping

condition (kuhn-DISH-uhn)--something that is needed before another thing can happen

covert (koh-VERT)--secret

disassemble (diss-uh-SEM-buhl)--take apart

freaky (FREE-kee)--very strange or abnormal

martian (MAWR-shuhn)--of or relating to the planet Mars or its supposed inhabitants

permission (per-MISH-uhn)--if you give permission for something, you say that you will allow it to happen

recognized (REK-uhg-nize)--to see someone and know who that person is

wonderland (WUHN-dur-land)--a place filled with wonders or surprises

VISUAL QUESTIONS & PROMPTS

1. Why do you think there's a panel border in the middle of this illustration? Does it make you read the panel differently? How does it make you feel?

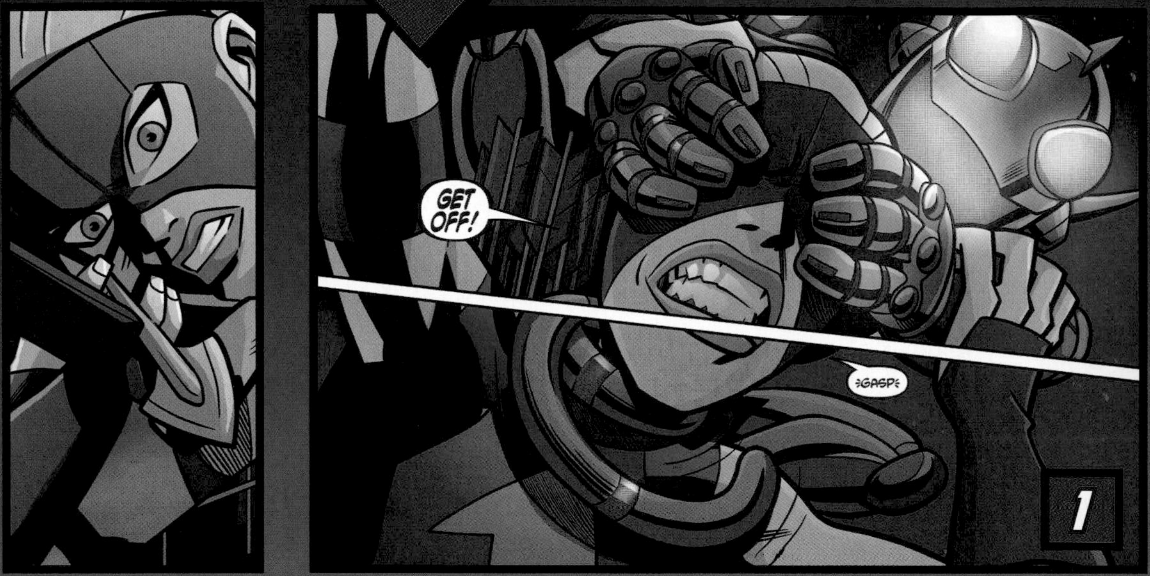
GET OFF!
GASP
1

2. Why might Artemis want to keep her private life a secret from the rest of the Young Justice team?

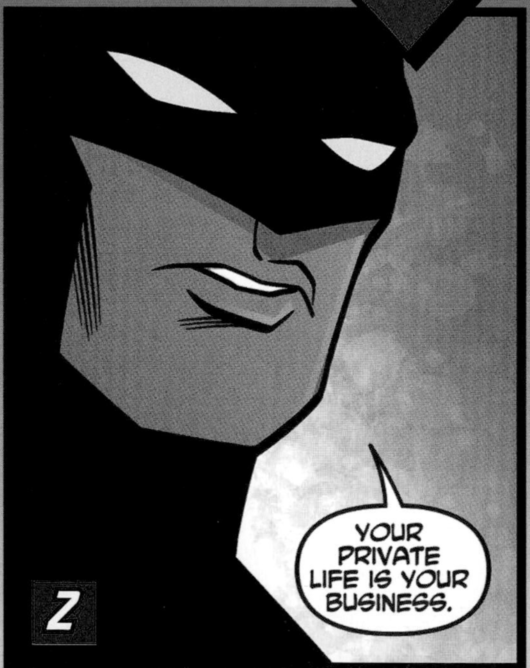
YOUR PRIVATE LIFE IS YOUR BUSINESS.
2

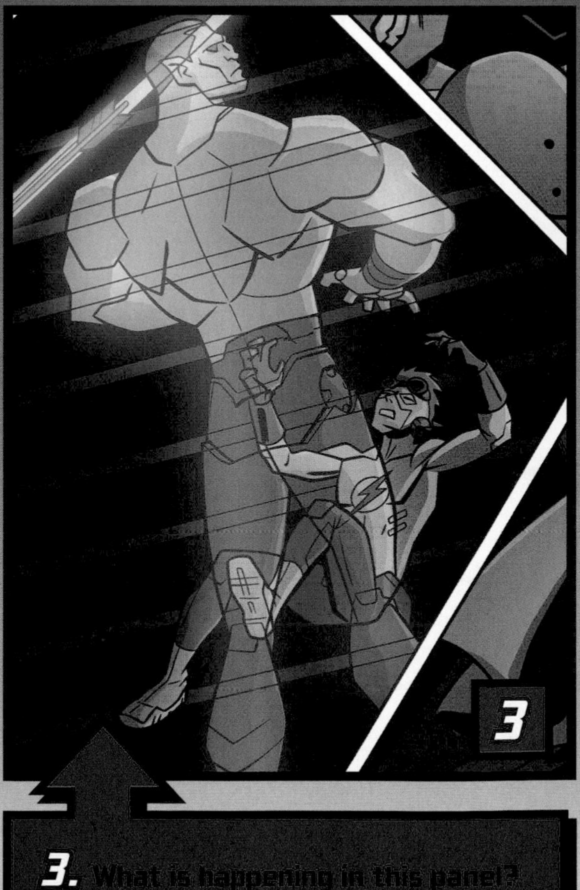
3

3. What is happening in this panel?

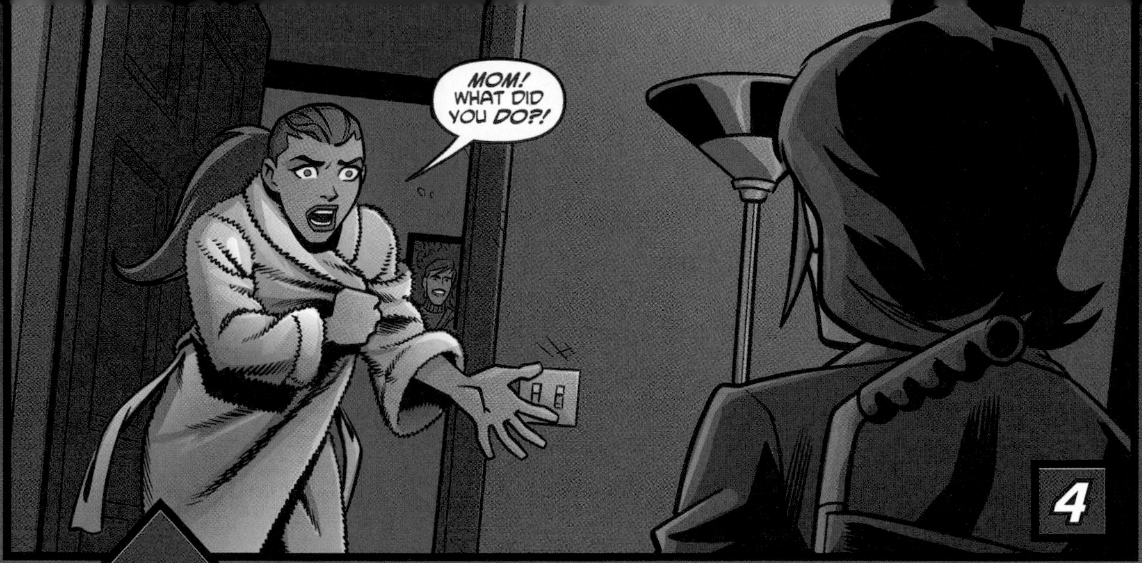
MOM! WHAT DID YOU DO?!
4

4. Why does Artemis think Batman and Green Arrow are there to see her mother?

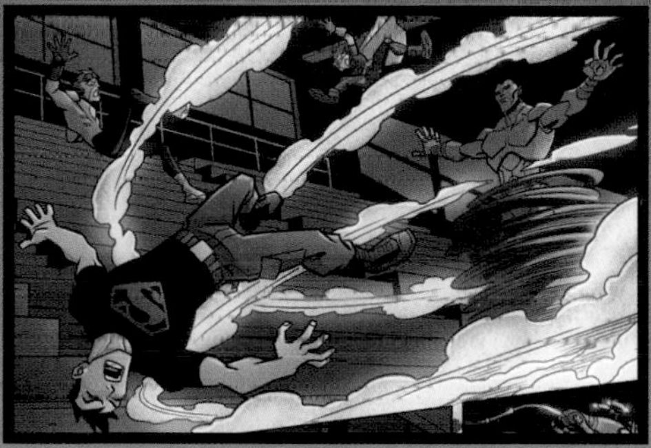

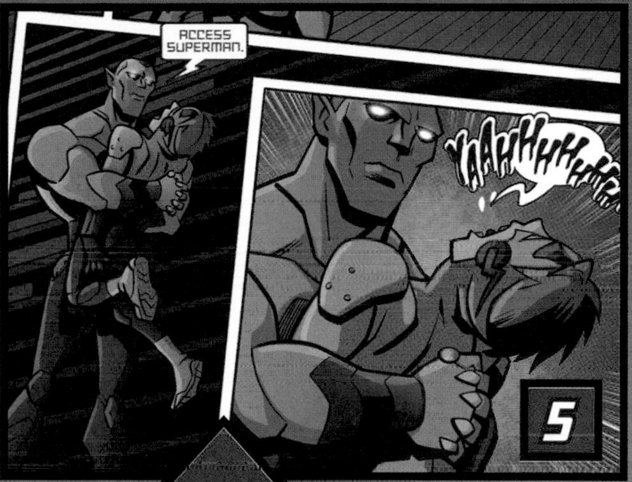
ACCESS SUPERMAN.
5

5. Based on this panel, what abilities or powers do you think this robot has?

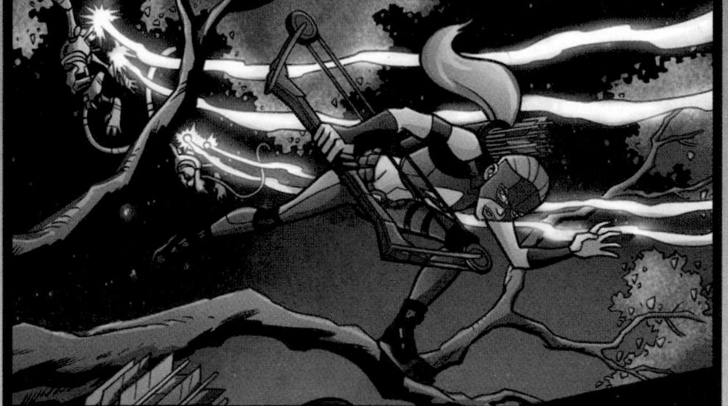

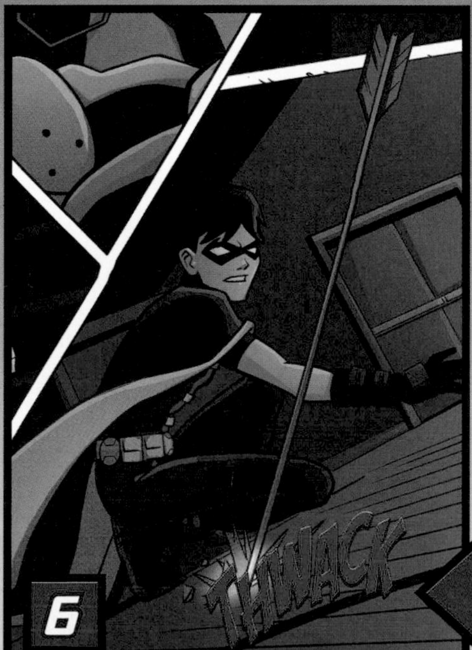
THWACK
6

6. How did Batman find out that Artemis was present at the scene of the fight?

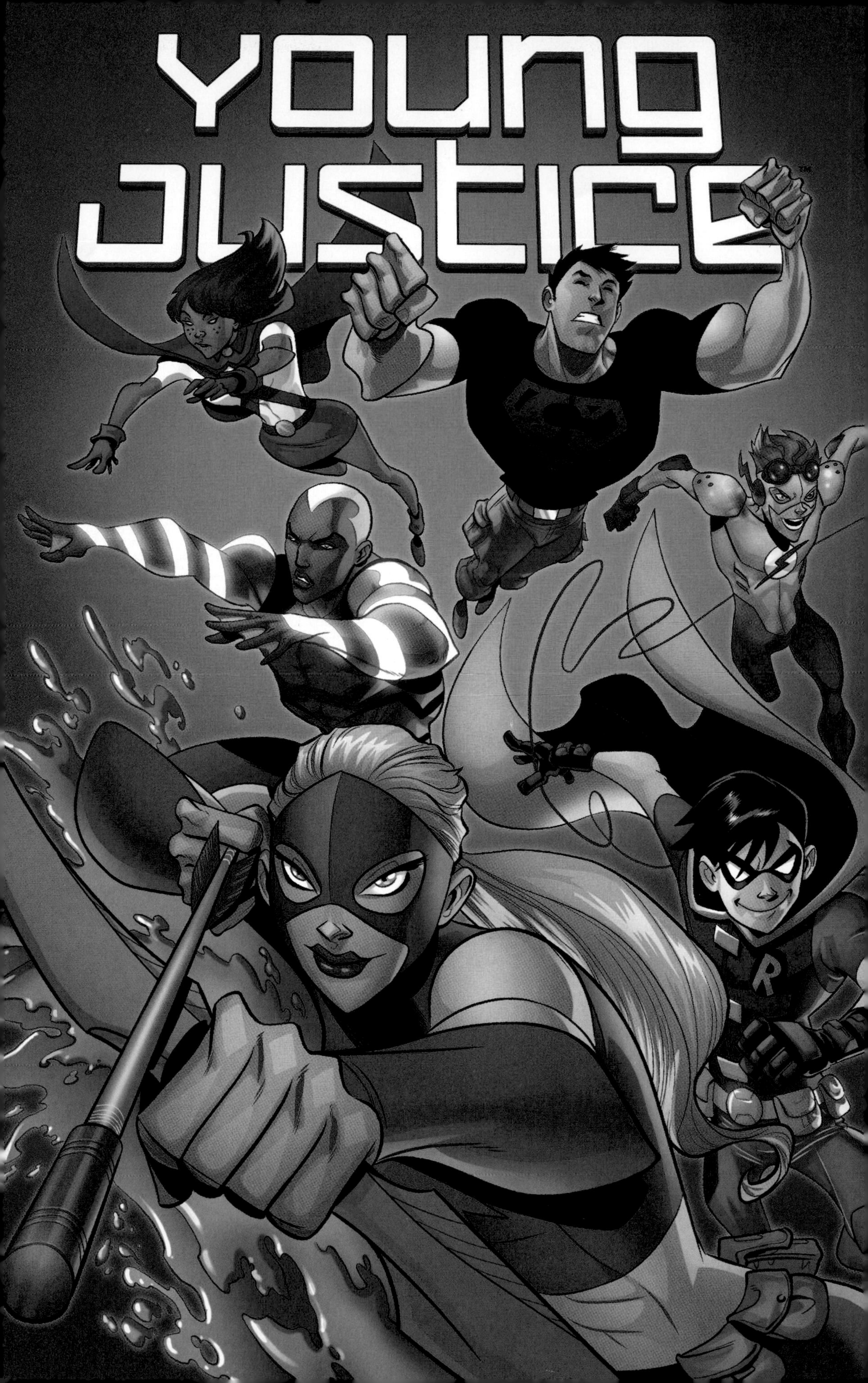
YOUNG
JUSTICE™